This book belongs to:

For Vicki, Lily, Edward and Tilly

Rockpool Children's Books
15 North Street
Marton
Warwickshire
CV23 9RJ

First published in Great Britain by Rockpool Children's Books Ltd. 2006
Text and Illustrations copyright © Stuart Trotter 2006
Stuart Trotter has asserted the moral rights
to be identified as the author and illustrator of this book.

ISBN 0-9553022-3-4
ISBN 978-0-9553022-3-7

Printed in China

Stuart Trotter

Boomerang Bear

rockpool
children's books

"I'm too big for Teddy,"
said Eddy.

So he threw him out of the window.

But Boomerang Bear came back.

He kicked him out of the door.

But Boomerang Bear came back.

Eddy flushed him down the toilet,
which was very naughty.

But Boomerang Bear came back.

He left him in the dark, dark woods.

But
Boomerang
Bear
came
back.

He tied him to
a rocket.

But Boomerang Bear
came back.

He left him
at the farm.

But Boomerang Bear came back.

He left him on
the ghost train.

But
Boomerang
Bear
came
back.

So Eddy sent
Teddy...

to Santa Claus.

And Boomerang Bear didn't come back.

He lost his appetite.

He drew pictures of
Teddy all day.
He wanted him back.

He couldn't sleep.
His bed seemed too
big and empty
without
Teddy.

Then came
Christmas Day.
Santa had left lots
of presents under
the tree.
One of them
caught Eddy's eye.

He ripped off
the wrapping
paper.

Boomerang Bear had come back!